IT WAS A BRIGHT SPRING MORNING
more than three hundred years ago.
There was great excitement in the little French town.
Children were screaming on their doorsteps.
Women were dashing towards the High Street.
Men, snatching up halberds and muskets,
joined the crowd
swarming around the Jolly Miller Inn.
They were ready for battle.

In those days panics were frequent.
France was at war with Spain.
The King schemed against his adviser, the Cardinal.
The Cardinal hatched plots against the King.
Gangs of thieves and beggars roamed the countryside.
So the townspeople always had their weapons ready
to deal with trouble of one kind or another.

THE THREE MUSKETEERS

Retold by Margaret Berrill
Illustrated by Susan Hunter

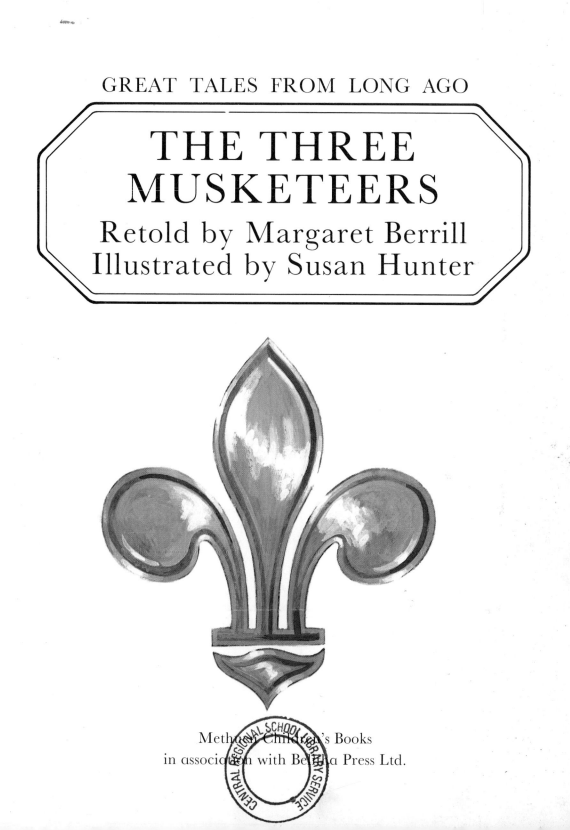

Methuen Children's Books
in association with Belitha Press Ltd.

Note: The text is based on part one of Lord
Sudley's translation of *The Three Musketeers*
by Alexandre Dumas (Penguin). Although
the King, Louis XIII, his Spanish Queen,
Anne of Austria, the Duke of Buckingham
and Cardinal Richelieu were real historical
figures, who lived in the first half of the
seventeenth century, Dumas wrote his story
more than two hundred years after the events
it describes. Names similar to those of
d'Artagnan and his three friends have been
traced, but very little is known about them,
and their story is largely drawn from Dumas'
imagination.

MB

Copyright © in this format Belitha Press Ltd, 1985
Text copyright © Margaret Berrill 1985
Illustrations copyright © Susan Hunter 1985
Art Director: Treld Bicknell
First published in Great Britain in 1985
by Methuen Children's Books Ltd,
11 New Fetter Lane, London EC4P 4EE
Conceived, designed and produced by Belitha Press Ltd,
2 Beresford Terrace, London N5 2DH
ISBN 0 416 53690 5 (hardback)
ISBN 0 416 54060 0 (paperback)
Printed by Purnell & Son (Book Production) Ltd,
Paulton, England

But today there was just one young man to deal with.
There he stood at the gate of the inn.
He was eighteen years old,
lanky, dark-haired and travel-stained.
He might have been a shabby farmer's son
except for the long sword he carried.
He had a proud, fierce look.
Beside him stood his horse,
an old yellow nag with a drooping head.

His horse was the cause of all the uproar.
Very funny it looked, and a gentleman
at the inn window was enjoying the joke.
The young man, whose name was d'Artagnan,
was deeply insulted.

"How dare you laugh at me, Sir?" he cried.
"I shall laugh whenever it suits me,"
replied the stranger scornfully.
D'Artagnan was enraged.
He drew his sword and lunged at the man.
Swiftly the innkeeper and two friends
attacked d'Artagnan with sticks, shovels and tongs.
He fell to the ground, dazed and bleeding,
and was carried into the inn.

WHEN HE CAME TO, D'ARTAGNAN LOOKED OUT OF THE WINDOW.
A beautiful lady was sitting in a coach.
The stranger was telling her,
"You must return to England, Milady.
Let the Cardinal know when the Duke leaves London."
Staggering outside, d'Artagnan cried,
"Now you shan't escape me, Sir!"
But the stranger swung into his saddle and was off.
The coachman whipped up his horses
and disappeared in the opposite direction.

SOON D'ARTAGNAN RECOVERED,
and was eager to get to Paris.
His greatest wish was to be a musketeer.
He had a letter for the Captain of Musketeers,
his father's friend.
He was furious to discover
that it had been stolen by the stranger.
He would not forget him or the beautiful Milady.
After a long tiring ride he reached Paris.

NEXT DAY, D'ARTAGNAN WENT TO THE HOUSE
of the Captain of Musketeers.
A rowdy crowd was gathered there.
The musketeers were brave and loyal.
Their job was to guard the King.
D'Artagnan wished that he still had the letter
because it might gain him the Captain's favour.

He was told that he must wait
and prove that he was fit to be a musketeer.
Three musketeers stood out from the crowd.
Their names were Athos, Porthos and Aramis.
D'Artagnan wished that he could be their friend.
But instead he annoyed each one in turn,
and each one challenged him to a duel.

D'Artagnan was sure
that one of the three musketeers would kill him.
They were expert swordsmen,
while he was little more than a boy.
But before the first duel could begin,
the three musketeers got into a fight
with five guardsmen, who were loyal to the Cardinal,
the King's adviser.

D'Artagnan fought like a lion on the musketeers' side.
Next day they got into another fight.
They wounded seven guardsmen in two days.

DUELLING WAS FORBIDDEN,
but secretly the King was pleased,
and rewarded d'Artagnan with gold.
D'Artagnan shared the gold with Athos, Porthos and Aramis.
They became great friends.
They shared everything they had.
Sometimes they had plenty of money.
Sometimes they were penniless and starving.
Then if one was invited out to dinner,
he took his three friends along.
"All for one, and one for all," they said.

THE MUSKETEERS SPENT THEIR TIME DRINKING AND GAMBLING.
D'Artagnan was bored.
He wanted to do brave deeds.
One day his landlord asked his help.
"My wife, Constance, has been kidnapped
by the Cardinal's men," he said.
"She is the Queen's dressmaker
and the Queen trusts her."

D'Artagnan knew the Queen was sad and lonely,
and that the King was unkind to her.
Her own country, Spain, was at war with France.
The Cardinal had set spies to watch her,
because he knew she was loved
by the Duke of Buckingham,
the most handsome and powerful man in England.
The Cardinal thought this was dangerous for the King
because France and England were enemies.

D'ARTAGNAN THOUGHT THAT THE KIDNAPPER sounded like the stranger who had stolen his letter. He must be a spy for the Cardinal. D'Artagnan agreed to help find Constance. Soon his landlord was arrested. The Cardinal's men waited in the landlord's room to trap visitors. Through a hole in the floorboards of his room above d'Artagnan listened.

ONE DAY HE HEARD A WOMAN'S SCREAMS. Constance had escaped from her kidnappers. D'Artagnan dashed down and rescued her from the Cardinal's men. "I must go," she said. "Please do not follow me. The Queen needs my help."

LATER IN THE DARK STREETS
d'Artagnan was amazed to see Constance
with a musketeer who looked like Aramis.
But he spoke with the voice of an Englishman.
The handsome musketeer
was the Duke of Buckingham in disguise.
He had been enticed to Paris by the Cardinal's men,
with a fake message from the Queen.
Now he was risking his life to see her,
with Constance's help.

D'Artagnan made sure that no danger befell
Constance and Buckingham.
In secret Buckingham met the Queen.
"Please return to England," she begged him,
"out of harm's way."
She gave him a gift, twelve diamond studs,
her birthday present from the King.
Then Constance guided him out of the palace.

THE CARDINAL WAS ANGRY WHEN HIS SPIES REPORTED
that Buckingham had seen the Queen.
He sent orders to his spy, Milady, in London.
She must steal two of the diamond studs
from the Duke of Buckingham.
He then persuaded the King to invite the Queen to a ball.
The King said, "You must be seen
wearing my present, the twelve diamond studs."

Alone again, the Queen wept bitterly.
"What am I to do?" she cried.
"The Cardinal must know everything!"
In despair she knelt on a cushion to pray.
"Perhaps I can help, Your Majesty," a gentle voice said.
Constance had been hanging up the Queen's dresses
when the King came in.
Hidden in the wardrobe, she had heard everything.
"Trust me," she went on.
"Write a letter to the Duke, and I will find someone
to take it to England."

CONSTANCE ASKED HER HUSBAND TO GO TO LONDON,
but he refused.
He had become a spy for the Cardinal.
D'Artagnan was eager to go.
He had heard them talking
through the hole in the floor.
D'Artagnan was sure the Cardinal would hear
about his journey, and try to stop him.
Athos, Porthos and Aramis remembered their motto,
"All for one, and one for all."
If all four set out, surely one would reach London
with the Queen's letter.
D'Artagnan was right.
Aramis was wounded in an ambush.
Porthos was trapped into a fight.
Noble Athos was accused of using forged money at an inn.

ONLY D'ARTAGNAN ESCAPED THE CARDINAL'S PLOTS
and crossed the sea to England.
"The Queen is in danger,"
he told the Duke of Buckingham.
"You must return the diamond studs."
Buckingham was horrified to find
that two of the studs were missing.
He guessed that Milady had stolen them.
But all was not lost.
Working day and night,
Buckingham's jeweller made two perfect copies.

BUCKINGHAM COMMANDED THAT NO SHIPS SHOULD LEAVE
English harbours for France.
A permit to leave was given to d'Artagnan.
As his boat left the Port of London,
he saw the beautiful Milady
seated in one of the boats waiting to leave for France.
A speedy crossing and a frantic ride
brought him to Paris by the night of the ball.

At THE BALL, THE QUEEN LOOKED VERY BEAUTIFUL.
The diamond studs on her shoulder
sparkled in the light of two hundred candles.
The Cardinal passed the King a box
containing the two studs brought by Milady.
"Ask the Queen who stole these from her," he said.
But when the King did so, the Queen showed him
that she was already wearing twelve studs.

The Cardinal had to pretend that he had bought
two extra studs as a gift for her.
"You are too generous, Sir," she said,
"for these two must have cost you as much
as the other twelve cost the King."
The Cardinal was furious.
He had been outwitted,
and the Queen saved from disgrace.

AFTER THE BALL, CONSTANCE LED D'ARTAGNAN
to a secret room.
There the Queen slipped into his hand
a diamond ring.
In his joy d'Artagnan knew
that there would be many other adventures
in which he and his three friends
would share their luck together,
daring any danger to protect the King and Queen.
And soon the day came when he had proved himself
fit to bear the name
of the King's Musketeers.